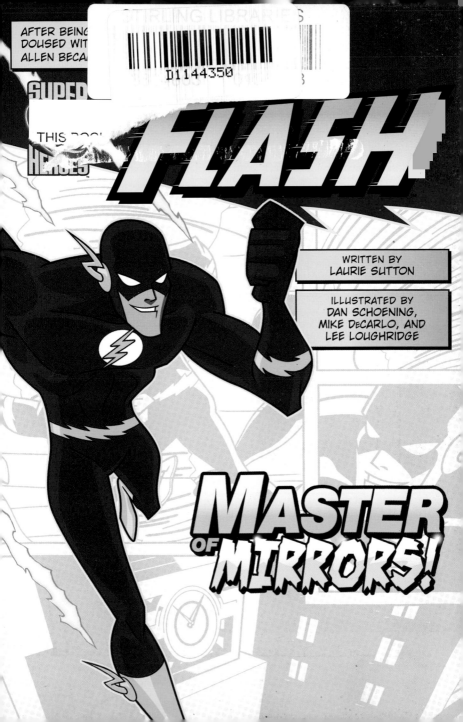

FLASH

MASTER OF MIRRORS!

WRITTEN BY
LAURIE SUTTON

ILLUSTRATED BY
DAN SCHOENING,
MIKE DeCARLO, AND
LEE LOUGHRIDGE

www.raintreepublishers.co.uk
Visit our website to find out
more information about
Raintree books.

To order:
☎ Phone 0845 6044371
🖨 Fax +44 (0) 1865 312263
✉ Email myorders@raintreepublishers.co.uk

Customers from outside the UK please telephone +44 1865 312262

Raintree is an imprint of Capstone Global Library Limited,
a company incorporated in England and Wales having its
registered office at 7 Pilgrim Street, London, EC4V 6LB –
Registered company number: 6695582

First published by Stone Arch Books in 2011
First published in the United Kingdom in 2012
The moral rights of the proprietor have been asserted.

The Flash and all related characters, names, and elements
are trademarks of DC Comics © 2011.

Art Director: Bob Lentz
Designer: Brann Garvey
Production Specialist: Michelle Biedscheid
Editor: Diyan Leake
Originated by Capstone Global Library Ltd
Printed and bound in China by Leo Paper Products Ltd

ISBN 978 1 406 23689 7
16 15 14 13 12 11
10 9 8 7 6 5 4 3 2 1

British Library Cataloguing in Publication Data
A full catalogue record for this book is available from the
British Library.

CONTENTS

CHAPTER 1

DAZZLE AND DASH

"Do diamonds come in purple?" the girl asked.

The jeweller gave the girl a puzzled look. "I've never been asked such an interesting question," he said.

"Mum doesn't want something that's purple," her brother said. "Just because *you* like purple –"

"Kids, we're here to get a gift for your mother," their father interrupted. "Please don't argue with each other."

"But shopping is boring, Dad!" the boy complained.

The jeweller handed a gold bracelet to the man. There was a small purple stone on it. "This is a very popular piece," he said.

"Hey, Dad!" the boy suddenly exclaimed. "Look at the super heroes!"

The man looked out the window where his son was pointing. Three men in colourful costumes were outside the jewellery shop. They were dressed exactly alike. Each one carried a bag. "I don't recognize them," the jeweller said.

"I thought the Flash was the only super hero in Central City," the dad added.

Just then, the trio of men burst into the jewellery shop. The boy's face lit up. "Are you guys members of the Justice League?"

The question made the men laugh. The boy frowned. The dad saw the unhappy look on his son's face. "You're not very friendly super heroes," he said.

"We're not super heroes at all," one of the men said, laughing even harder. "We're super-*villains*!"

"And this is a robbery!" the second one added.

"Open up all your jewellery cases," the third man said to the jeweller.

The jeweller was forced to obey. Each of the identical thieves grabbed necklaces and rings and bracelets made of diamonds. It took them only a minute to fill their bags with loot. Then they rushed out the door.

As soon as the robbers were gone, the jeweller hit the alarm. **BEEP! BEEP!**

The alarm was so loud that the dad and his kids had to cover their ears.

Outside on the street the three villains paid no attention to the alarm. They did not run away from the shop they had just robbed. The sounds of police sirens came closer and closer, but the crooks stayed calm. One of them took out a roll of silver plastic and spread open the sheet on the ground. It looked just like a mirror.

"Let's go, boys," he told the others. The thief jumped onto the surface of the bright plastic and suddenly disappeared into it! It was as if he had jumped down a hole in the ground. The other two robbers followed and vanished as well.

Police cars screeched to a stop in front of the jewellery shop. The officers ran into the shop, ignoring the sheet of plastic.

They did not know that the thieves had used it to escape. Moments later, it blew away in the breeze.

*   *   *

Meanwhile, on the other side of town, Barry Allen stood in front of a department shop window. He was taking a break from his duties as the Flash. Even though he was secretly the Fastest Man Alive, it was taking him a long time to finish shopping. *Maybe I should go shopping as the Flash next time,* Barry thought.

Suddenly, Barry saw a reflection in the department store window. Three men in identical costumes appeared out of nowhere! The men were entering a building across the street – an expensive art gallery.

This looks like trouble, Barry decided.

Barry pressed a secret switch on his ring. **POOF!** His Flash uniform burst out from a hidden compartment. He was a super-speedy blur as he became the Flash.

The three thieves from the jewellery shop stood in the art gallery. One of them pointed at a painting. "We'll take the Picasso," he told the gallery owner.

"The Master likes that one," the second crook said.

"He likes the mirror in it," the third said.

The owner was not sure about these costumed customers. No one had ever come into the gallery dressed so strangely before.

"An excellent choice," he said nervously. "Will you be paying by cheque?"

"We won't be paying at all," the third thief said.

The first thief took the painting off the wall and walked towards the door. "Wait a minute. You can't do that!" the clerk said. "Just who do you people think you are?!"

ZOOOM! Suddenly, the Flash stood between the thieves and the exit.

"They're not people," the Flash said. "They're copies of the Mirror Master!"

"Actually, I prefer the term *replica*," the first crook said.

"We're clones," the second one said.

"I like mirror minions," the third said.

"You'll all be called *jailbirds* in a moment," the Flash announced.

The duplicates did not seem worried. "If we're caught, the Master will just make more of us," one of them said, shrugging.

"But we're not going to be caught!" the clones said together.

All three thieves touched the mirror in the painting. Suddenly, they were inside it! A moment later, they had disappeared into the painting's background. The piece of art was normal again.

"The Mirror Master is back," the Flash said. "But what is he up to this time?"

CHAPTER 2

MIRROR MASTER

The Flash was patrolling Central City, on high alert for the Mirror Master. The sneaky super-villain had the power to use mirrors in many ways. He could use something called the Mirror Dimension to walk into any mirror like it was a door and come out of another mirror anywhere in the world.

He could also make living duplicates of his own reflection as long as he remained inside the Mirror Dimension. The Flash had seen both of those powers in action at the art gallery.

Suddenly, Flash saw police cars speed down the street. The sirens were going full-blast and the lights were flashing. The Flash followed them until they all stopped at the same place – the Central City Bank.

WHOOOOSH!

The Flash ran into the bank and looked for the Mirror Master and his duplicates. There was no sign of them. A super-villain was not causing the trouble at the bank. It was just a normal criminal.

"Put your hands up," an officer warned.

The robber did not obey the command.

The Flash ran up to the police officer. "Let me help," he said.

When the bank robber spotted the Flash by the officer, he quickly put his hands in the air. "I surrender!" he said.

"It looks like you already helped, Flash!" the officer said.

BZZT! A message came over the officer's radio. "There's a monster in Central City Park!" the dispatcher said. "All units please respond!"

"That sounds like a job for the Flash," the officer said. He turned back to where the Flash had been, but the Scarlet Speedster was already gone.

Flash zoomed his way into the Central City Park. Everything about the park was beautiful this time of year – everything except for . . . a monster! The creature looked like a broken mirror put back together, the edges as sharp as swords.

"That's definitely the work of the Mirror Master," Flash said.

The monster was stomping through the park. It didn't seem to care where it was going. The Flash saw that people were in danger. He ran back and forth between the crowds and the monster, creating a wall of wind. The mirror monster bumped up against the barrier.

CRUNCH! Parts of the creature broke away from its body.

That gave Flash an idea. At super-speed, Flash started to spin like a top. He spun faster and faster, until he became a red and gold tornado.

The mirror monster got sucked into the whirlwind. It twisted around and around. The force of the wind inside the vortex grew stronger. The creature shattered into pieces. Then the pieces smashed together, grinding themselves into tiny bits.

The Flash stopped spinning. The monster had been reduced to a giant pile of sand – the basic material that mirrors are made of. The kids in the park cheered for the Flash.

The Flash looked around with narrowed eyes. "Where is Mirror Master?" he said. "He sent this creature for a reason."

The Flash did not have to look very far. He saw three bright sports cars speeding down the street. The drivers were Mirror Master's copies. *They probably stole the cars while I was distracted with fighting the monster,* he thought.

WHOOOOSH!

The Flash rushed towards the rear car. The driver did not notice the Flash was behind him because he was too busy checking his reflection in his mirror.

Flash ran up alongside the car. "You're as vain as your boss," the Flash said.

The mirror duplicate was surprised to see the Flash running next to the car. The driver swerved and stepped on the accelerator. The car zoomed up the street. When the crook peered over his left shoulder to look for the Flash, he did not see the hero.

"Ha!" the thief said. "I lost him!"

"No, you didn't," the Flash replied. He was sitting in the passenger seat of the car. "I think this test drive is over."

But instead of stopping, the mirror thief sped up. The car raced towards a building at the end of the street. In front of them, the other stolen cars were doing the same thing. It looked as if they were going to crash into the building!

Flash could do nothing but watch. He didn't want to put the driver, or anyone else, at risk.

The cars rushed towards the large window on the front of the building. The Flash could see their reflections in it. The first car hit the glass, but there was no crash – the car just disappeared! Then the second car did the same.

"It's a portal," the Flash said. "Just like the mirror in that painting."

Then the car with the Flash inside passed into the glass window portal.

CHAPTER 3

INTO THE LOOKING GLASS

The three sports cars emerged on the other side of the mirror portal. Their tyres skidded over cobblestones. RUMMMMMMMMBLE! They did not slow down. Flash caught a glimpse of people running away from the roaring vehicles. Everyone wore simple, strange clothing.

Flash looked up at the green sky and yellow clouds. *We're not in Central City any more*, the hero said to himself.

"We're in another dimension," the driver said.

"It's just like Alice going into the looking glass!" he added. Then, he slammed on the brakes. **SKKRREEEEEE**

The Flash was thrown forwards in his seat. **WHAM!** "Ow," Flash said. "That'll remind me to fasten my seatbelt."

The mirror thief pulled out a laser blaster and pointed it at the Flash, but he didn't get a chance to fire it. **THWACK!** Flash knocked it from his hand in a split second. The Flash was surprised at what happened when his hand hit the thief's arm. The mirror duplicate shattered!

"I guess they don't make evil minions like they used to," Flash joked.

The other two stolen cars sped through the streets of the village. It would be easy for the Flash to stop them, but he didn't.

Flash wanted the crooks to lead him to the Mirror Master. Otherwise, these doubles would return to run wild in Central City.

The cars drove towards a giant stone castle that looked like something out of a fantasy game. There were turrets, a moat, and a drawbridge. The crooks drove over the drawbridge and through a huge gate. They finally stopped in a large courtyard lined with knights in shining armour. All the knights looked identical.

"More mirror minions," Flash said. "This must be Mirror Master's fortress."

"Hey! It's the Flash!" one of the car thieves said. "How'd he get here?"

"Who cares?!" the other thief shouted. "Guards, seize him!" The knights surrounded the Flash.

The knights' armour was so highly polished that the sun's light reflected off it and blinded him. **WHOOOOSH!** Flash narrowly dodged a battle-axe that rushed past his head. The knights attacked the Flash with swords and long spears. The hero remembered how the mirror thief had shattered when he was hit. The Flash punched the nearest knight at super-speed.

CRUNCH! The knight cracked and fell into a thousand pieces.

The Flash used his fists like pistons to smash the other mirror knights. He ran around the whole courtyard and broke them all to pieces. **SMASH!** When he finally stopped punching, there were heaps of broken glass everywhere.

"That's seven years of bad luck for me," Flash said, chuckling to himself.

He turned to the pair of car thieves. One of them was foolish enough to pull a weapon on the Flash. It took less than a millisecond for the Flash to respond.

WHAM! The crook became a pile of broken shards on the ground.

"Where's the Mirror Master?" Flash asked the last mirror thief.

"In . . . in the throne room," he said nervously.

"Take me to him," Flash ordered. *"Now!"*

The crook obeyed and led the Flash into the castle. There were no more knights to stand in the way. They walked down a hall lined with mirrors on both sides. Mirrors covered the floor and ceiling, too. Their reflections stared back at them from every direction.

Each piece of art hanging on the walls had a mirror theme. *That's why Mirror Master wanted to steal that mirror painting,* Flash thought. *He was designing his secret base!*

At the end of the hall of mirrors stood a tall door of polished metal. The Flash could see himself in it. The minion pushed it open. On the other side was the throne room and sitting on a throne was the Mirror Master.

"Now this is a surprise," Mirror Master said. "I was expecting my minions to return with loot, not with the Scarlet Speedster himself!"

The Flash looked around the room. Everything was made of mirrors. "The place looks like the inside of a giant disco ball!" Flash joked.

The villain ignored him. He turned towards a woman sitting on a stool next to him. Her dress was covered in diamonds. The Flash wondered if the jewels were stolen like the paintings and the cars.

"This is my princess," Mirror Master said. "You should have seen how boring she looked before I made her this new outfit."

"*Princess*?" Flash repeated, confused.

The woman looked at the Flash but did not speak. Her eyes were very sad.

"She's such a sweet thing," Mirror Master said. "Her people will do anything to keep her safe – like making me king!"

He rose from his throne. "Welcome to my kingdom, Flash," he bellowed. "I call it Mirror World!"

CHAPTER 4

TRAPPED IN MIRROR WORLD

"You shouldn't have come here, Flash," said the Mirror Master. "You always interfere with my plans!"

"Your plans tend to hurt people," the Flash replied. "It's my job to protect them."

The Flash looked at the sad princess. He noticed that her wrists were bound together with thick silver chains. Her mouth moved to form silent words: "Help me."

"I'm taking great care of Princess Oriana," Mirror Master said.

He gestured at the captive. "See how pretty she is in all these diamonds?"

"Those diamonds are stolen, just like this kingdom," Flash said. "Your reign is over."

"Not without a fight," Mirror Master promised. Suddenly, a hundred duplicates of Flash jumped out of the mirrors. They surrounded the super hero.

"More mirror minions?" Flash said. "You should call yourself Copycat Master, not Mirror Master."

"I'm the Mirror *King*, now," the villain boasted. "Seize him, my minions!"

The duplicates reached for the Flash. He shattered the nearest ones with his fists, but more kept coming. **KRAK! BANG!**

Flash kept breaking them. Soon, he was surrounded by heaps of jagged glass.

The Mirror Master sat on his throne and laughed. "The more you break, the more I make," he said. "I can do this all day!"

Twenty mirror duplicates grabbed at the Flash. They held his arms and legs. He could not move or fight back.

"Surrender, Flash!" Mirror Master said.

"Giving up is not in my job description," Flash answered.

The Flash began to concentrate. He did not appear to be moving, but his molecules were vibrating at incredible speed. The vibrations spread down the arms of the mirror duplicates who held him. CRASH! They exploded, bursting into fine grains of sand.

"I'm making quite a mess in here," Flash said. "Let me clean it up."

The Flash ran around at super-speed, causing the shards to spin around the room. They hit the mirrors on the walls, shattering them. **CRASH!!** The minions and mirrors all broke. It was like being caught in a crazy snow globe.

At last, the Flash stopped. The mirrors were gone. Now, the room was bare stone.

"Surrender, villain," the Flash said.

"That's not in my job description, either," the villain answered. He pointed a wand at the Flash. There was a little mirror on the tip. The light in the room made it sparkle and pulse. The Flash could not take his eyes away from it.

"I command you to stand still!" Mirror Master said. The Flash obeyed. He stood motionless before the Mirror Master.

"You've put a spell on him!" Princess Oriana cried out in surprise.

"I've hypnotized him," Mirror Master said. "Not magic – just light and mirrors."

Mirror Master waved the wand at his foe. "I am the king," Mirror Master said. "And every king needs a court jester!"

Mirror Master waved his wand once more. "Dance, Flash!" he said.

The Flash started to dance. "Now, Flash," the villain added, "stand on your head!"

The Flash turned himself upside down.

"And sing," Mirror Master said.

"Mary had a little lamb, little lamb," Flash sang. "With fleece as white as snow."

"Stop!" Mirror Master complained. "You have a terrible singing voice."

The Flash stopped singing. He still stood on his head. "This isn't as fun as I imagined," Mirror Master decided.

Oriana shook her head sadly.

"You were hoping he'd save you," Mirror Master said. "You hoped he'd be the knight in shining armour riding in to rescue the kidnapped princess, just like in a fairy tale. But I'm afraid this fairy tale won't have a happy ending."

The Mirror Master stomped out of the throne room. He left the Flash standing on his head.

"I don't know what a fairy tale is," Oriana whispered. "But I believe the Flash will save me!"

If only I knew how to break the spell on him! thought the princess.

CHAPTER 5

JOUST IN TIME

The Mirror Master was not happy that the Flash had smashed all his mirror knights. He made a new troop of knights that surrounded the Flash. They walked him out onto a grassy field.

The people from the village stood behind colourful ropes along both sides of the field. Mirror knights forced the audience to cheer by threatening them with their swords.

The Mirror Master made a grand entrance. He wore a royal crown and a fancy cape.

Next to him was Princess Oriana. The cheers turned into silence. The people did not like seeing their princess as a captive.

"My subjects!" the Mirror Master announced. "Witness what happens to the enemies of Mirror World."

He pointed to the Flash. The hero was now wearing a suit of red armour. A yellow lightning design was on the breastplate. He had no weapons. The Flash stood like a statue. He was still hypnotized by the Mirror Master.

"I call my champions to the field of battle," Mirror Master said.

Suddenly, two knights riding mirror monsters charged towards the Flash. They carried jousting spears. The spears were aimed directly at the Flash's chest.

The crowd became restless. They could see what was going to happen. If the red knight did not move, he would be killed. They yelled for him to move, but he didn't.

Princess Oriana put her hands to her cheeks in fear. "It's not a spell," she said to herself. "It's just mirrors and light . . ."

Oriana moved her dress so that the diamonds on it threw reflected light into the Flash's eyes. The dazzle made him blink. Suddenly, he was awake!

The Flash dodged the two knights charging towards him. He felt awkward in the suit of heavy armour, but it did not slow him down. KRASSSHHH! The jousting knights slammed into each other.

"What the –?!" Mirror Master sputtered. "Mirror knights, stop him!"

The duplicates ran at the Flash with their swords raised. The Flash clapped his hands together at super-speed.

The shock waves of sound hit the nearest knights. They exploded. The Flash waited for another wave of mirror knights to attack, but they never came. The villagers had seen him shatter the knights and had done the same to the remaining minions. There were no more knights left!

"You really know how to ruin a party, Flash," Mirror Master said. The villain pointed the hypno-wand at the Flash. The mirror spun. Light sparkled and pulsed.

The Flash held up his mirror sword. The light from the wand reflected back to the Mirror Master.

The villain could not take his eyes away from it. "I command you to surrender," Flash said.

The villain obeyed. He had been hypnotized by his own wand.

"You have saved us all, Flash," Princess Oriana said. "You are our hero!"

"It wasn't me," the Flash replied. "You saved my life, remember? If it weren't for you, I never would've beaten this villain."

The princess blushed and smiled at the compliment. Flash took her silver chains in his hands and rubbed the metal at super-speed. **CLANK!** The friction made the silver soft enough to pull the links apart. The princess turned to face her subjects. She spread her arms to show them that she was free. A mighty cheer went up.

"Hooray for the Red Knight!" they shouted.

"From this day forwards, you shall be known as Sir Flash, the Red Knight," Princess Oriana declared. She took the mirror sword from the Flash. "Please kneel, Sir Flash."

The Flash bent down on one knee. Oriana touched the blade of the sword on his shoulder. "I name you Hero of our Realm," she said. "Defender of the weak, vanquisher of the cruel."

"Hooray for Sir Flash!" the crowd yelled.

The villagers danced and ate and sang songs late into the day. They were happy that their princess was safe and that everyone was free from the Mirror Master. The royal realm was back to normal.

*   *   *

After the celebration, Princess Oriana stood beside the mirror portal in the village square to say goodbye to the Flash. The Mirror Master was in iron chains. All the stolen paintings and loot were piled up in the three sports cars. The Flash pushed them through the portal carefully.

"I'll make sure everything is returned to the rightful owners," Flash said.

"What about him?" the princess asked, pointing at Mirror Master. "He must be punished so he will learn his lesson."

"Don't worry about that," Flash said. "Where Mirror Master is headed, he'll have plenty of time to *reflect* on his mistakes."

"Is this the end of the fairy tale?" the princess asked.

"I'm afraid so," Flash replied. "But at least this one has a happy ending."

"Will we ever see you again?" she asked.

"No, Your Highness," Flash said. "After I leave, you must break the glass portal so no one can ever come back here. Otherwise, you will not be safe."

"I understand," she said. "And I will never forget you."

"I will never forget you, either," Flash said. He stepped through the portal with the Mirror Master following him obediently. Princess Oriana smiled when she saw the Flash turn back and wave a final goodbye.

"Farewell, Sir Flash," she whispered.

KRASSHH! She swung her sword and smashed the mirror to bits.

○ ○ ○   MIRROR MASTER

MIRROR MASTER

REAL NAME: EVAN McCULLOCH

OCCUPATION: PROFESSIONAL CRIMINAL

HEIGHT: 1.80 METRES

WEIGHT: 78 KG

EYES: BROWN

HAIR: BROWN

SPECIAL POWERS/ABILITIES:
Maintains an arsenal of reflective weapons; able to turn an enemy's reflection against them; able to trap opponents in mirrors; can transport himself from one mirror to another through the "Mirror Dimension".

done

MIRROR MASTER BIO

BIOGRAPHY:

Growing up an orphan, Evan McCulloch had a childhood that was nothing to reflect upon. Abused and bullied from an early age, the wild-eyed teen eventually turned to a life of crime – and discovered a knack for it. Soon, his shady skills captured the attention of the US government. They wanted McCulloch to work for good instead of evil. As an incentive, they gave the criminal the uniform of a deceased super-villain, the Mirror Master. McCulloch embraced the role too well, becoming a super-villain himself.

MIRROR MASTER FACTS

Mirror Master is a member of the Rogues, a criminal organization led by Captain Cold.

Other Rogue members include Weather Wizard, Trickster, Captain Boomerang, and Heatwave.

The original Mirror Master, Samuel Joseph Scudder, invented the high-tech uniform.

BIOGRAPHIES

Laurie Sutton has read comic books since she was a child. She grew up to become an editor for Marvel, DC Comics, Starblaze, and Tekno Comics. She has written *Adam Strange* for DC, *Star Trek: Voyager* for Marvel, plus *Star Trek: Deep Space Nine* and *Witch Hunter* for Malibu Comics. There are boxes of comics in her wardrobe where there should be clothes and shoes. Laurie has lived all over the world.

Erik Doescher is a freelance illustrator and video game designer. He illustrated for a number of comic studios throughout the 1990s, and then moved into video game development and design. However, he has not given up on illustrating his favourite comic book characters.

Mike DeCarlo is a contributor of comic art whose range extends from Batman and Iron Man to Bugs Bunny and Scooby-Doo.

Lee Loughridge has been working in comics for more than fifteen years. He currently lives in a tent on the beach.

GLOSSARY

clone plant or animal from the cells of a parent or animal that is identical to the parent

cobblestone flat, round grey rock once used to pave roads

hypnotize place under a spell

loot stolen money or valuables

moat deep, wide ditch dug around a castle and filled with water to prevent attacks

Picasso a painter and sculptor from France who lived from 1881 to 1973

portal door or entrance

replica exact copy of something

vain conceited or proud of oneself

vortex swirling body of water that looks like an underwater tornado

DISCUSSION QUESTIONS

1. At the end of the story, Flash says the Mirror Master will be punished. What do you think would be the best punishment for the villain?

2. In this book, Flash wears two different uniforms. Which one do you like better, and why?

3. The Flash has super-speed. Mirror Master has the power to control mirrors. Which superpower would you rather have? Why?

WRITING PROMPTS

1. In this adventure, the Flash gets a new uniform. Create your own Flash uniform. Describe its powers and the material it's made from. Then draw a picture of the uniform.

2. Write another story where the Flash takes on the Mirror Master. Where will they battle next time? Who will win? The choice is up to you.

3. Imagine you could jump into your bathroom mirror and come out another mirror anywhere in the world. Where would you travel to? Write a story about your adventure.

MORE NEW

ADVENTURES!

CAPTAIN BOOMERANG'S
COMEBACK!

CLOCK KING'S
TIME BOMB

TRICKSTER'S BUBBLE
TROUBLE

KILLER KALEIDOSCOPE

ICE AND FLAME